KING
of the
BENCH
NO FEAR!

STEVE MOORE

HARPER
An Imprint of HarperCollinsPublishers

ISBN 978-0-06-220330-4

Typography by Katie Klimowicz
17 18 19 20 21 CG/LSCH 1 2 3 4 5 6 7 8 9 10

To my Mom and Dad

PROLOGUE

My name is Steve, and I am a bench-warmer.

I "sit the pine," as coaches like to say. But it doesn't bother me all that much. I figure it's probably just one of those tough phases that most people go through, like zits or algebra.

Don't feel all sorry for me when I say this, but no matter the sport, coaches never put me in a game unless it's garbage time and the score is a hundred to zip.

Mostly I sit on the bench with my friends Carlos and Joey and watch the hotshot athletes run around and sweat like pigs just to impress the girls. You probably already know this, but sweat is a huge chick magnet.

I go to Spiro T. Agnew Middle School, "Home of the Mighty Plumbers." Yeah, our mascot is a plumber. I guess the image of a guy in overalls holding a pipe wrench is supposed to strike fear in the hearts of our opponents.

Derp!

I'm not a drooling dweeb, okay? I've got some important skills. For example, I'm very quick on my feet. That's really handy in football when a linebacker is trying to grab your head and shove your face into the grass.

I'm also pretty good at passing a basketball. My specialty is tossing the ball back inbounds after someone scores a basket. I hardly ever toss it to the wrong person by accident.

And in baseball I can slide into a bag better than anyone else my age. I slide headfirst or feetfirst. Doesn't matter. I pretty much rule sliding.

No brag. It's just a fact.

I use my skills in things other than sports, too.

In school my quick feet help me to dodge through the hallway traffic jam between classes when I desperately need to use the restroom.

My passing skills are crucial in class when I need to throw a bag of Reese's Pieces to a buddy on the other side of the room.

And my excellent sliding ability?

One time I was running in the cafeteria with my food tray, which is strictly forbidden. I slipped on spilled spaghetti, but I didn't fall and crack my skull open, because I dropped into sliding position and skidded across the linoleum floor . . .

. . . right into a stack of milk cartons.

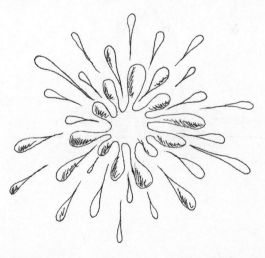

Everyone in the cafeteria gave me a standing ovation. It was awesome.

So yeah, I'm a benchwarmer, but don't feel sorry for me. I actually like sitting the pine.

Benchwarmers like me observe life from just the right angle. I'm not sitting too high up, where I look down on the rest of the world like Jimmy Jimerino.

Jimmy Jimerino is the Spiro T. Agnew BJOC—Big Jock on Campus. Every school's got one.

Jimmy gets whatever he wants and never gets in trouble no matter how many tests he flunks or rules he breaks. He's got a hall pass for life simply because he's great at sports.

Not all the hotshot athletes at my school are like Jimmy, though.

Becky O'Callahan is way better at sports than Jimmy Jimerino, but she doesn't have the BJOC attitude.

Becky is friendly to everyone, even if they don't happen to be athletes. And she gets good grades and never gets in trouble.

From my view on the bench I also get to see things that no one else sees, like my baseball coach's amazing habit.

All game long he digs huge chunks of wax out of his ears with a car key, and then he rolls them up and sticks the wads under the bench like chewing gum. His head is practically a wax factory!

I call him Coach Earwax.

But this book is about more than just earwax or BJOC or plumbers or even Becky O'Callahan.

I'm writing about my very first baseball season at Spiro T. Agnew Middle School, and a really humiliating personal problem that almost ruined it.

No, not that.

I developed Bean-O-Phobia. It's a crippling fear of getting hit by a pitch.

If you've ever had Bean-O-Phobia you

know how traumatic life can be. I mean, how can you be a baseball player if you're afraid of the ball?

You might be wondering why I'd write a book and tell total strangers all about being a benchwarmer and the humiliating phobia that almost ruined my life.

Duh. It's pretty much a rule that you spill your guts when you write a book about yourself.

If my story helps just one person with Bean-O-Phobia, then it'll be worth all the humiliation.

And you know what? I don't even want to be like Jimmy Jimerino.

When you're a BJOC, you've got to win at everything, and who needs that kind of pressure?

Besides, when it comes to sitting on the bench, I'm probably better at it than anyone else my age in the entire city—maybe the entire world.

End of the pine. Middle of the pine. Doesn't matter. I pretty much rule the bench.

No brag. It's just a fact.

I'm King of the Bench!

CHAPTER 1

I'll take you back to when it all began.

I have played sports my whole life, but this year was different. This was the year I tried out for the Spiro T. Agnew Middle School baseball team.

Yeah, that's right. There was a tryout.

In my town, youth sports are different than school sports. In youth sports, every kid gets on a team and every kid plays and every kid gets a trophy. No losers. Ever!

Anyone who walks onto the field with a pulse is guaranteed to get on a team and play.

But once you're done with youth sports and want to play for a school, there's only one option:

Try out for the team and risk total rejection.

Just when all those unathletic kids start thinking that maybe they could someday be professional athletes and earn billions of dollars, cruel reality whacks them upside the head.

Team tryouts are a major milestone in life—even bigger than when you get toilet trained.

It's a game changer. If you can't run or throw or catch or hit a baseball, then you get cut. It's survival of the fittest!

Team tryouts are as old as humanity, by the way.

There are Stone Age cave drawings in France that show early humans trying out for teams that hunted woolly mammoths. The competition was intense. Hunters who couldn't throw spears were humiliated—and they missed out on an excellent feast of barbecued mammoth ribs.

NERD.

I hoped trying out for the middle school baseball team wouldn't be quite as brutal, but I was determined to take a risk. And either way, whenever I want to do something with any kind of risk, I need to clear it with the "Power Structure."

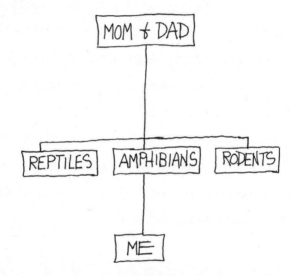

I asked my dad for permission first because I knew he'd be excited about me trying out for the Mighty Plumbers baseball team. Dad was a hotshot athlete before he ruined his knees in college, so he supports any kind of sports activity.

I think he secretly hopes that a miracle will happen and I'll suddenly blossom into a hotshot athlete, but in the meantime he is really supportive. He always says, "It doesn't matter if you hardly play. What matters is that you play hard."

Mom was a different story.

I guess she feared that *school* baseball would be more dangerous than *youth* base-ball. Somehow the game would morph into something deadly.

SCREAMING LINE DRIVES!! WICKED HOPS!!! WILD PITCHES!!!!

Part of Mom's problem is that I'm an only child. And yeah. I already know what you're thinking: Steve plays the violin or is a spoiled brat. Probably both.

But you'd be wrong. Those are only-child stereotypes.

I'm about as musical as a dirt clod.

'BANG THE TAMBOURINE REPEATEDLY AGAINST YOUR PALM AND'...WHA??

HOW TO PLAY THE TAMBOURINE

And I'm not a spoiled brat, either. I can prove it.

You know how rats always die in the attic and stink up your entire house? It's really rank. Well, I'm the one in our family who always has to crawl up into the attic to get rid of the body.

How many spoiled brats do you know who will even *look* at the rotting corpse of a rat?

Mom is overprotective, though, and that's an only-child stereotype that happens to be true. In fact, Mom is an overprotective turbo-hyper-worrywart, and I'm not even exaggerating.

Here's an example: when I entered junior high and started walking to school instead of taking the bus, Mom actually wanted me to wear a helmet. A *helmet*!

I could understand if I was riding a skateboard or a Harley-Davidson. But a helmet? For *walking*?

Luckily, Dad stepped in and talked her out of it.

Sometimes Mom can be pretty cool about the whole hovering thing, though.

Last year in youth basketball, I didn't get to play until the final three seconds of a game—even though we were winning by about a hundred points and it was the last game of the season.

I could tell Mom felt bad for me and wanted to hover and be all gooey and mushy right in front of my teammates. But she waited until we were in the car so I wouldn't be embarrassed, *then* she gave me a kiss and a mushy hug.

When moms do things like that, you can almost put up with them doing gross things like kissing you on the cheek and then wiping the lipstick off your face with their germy spit.

Anyway, when I told Mom that I wanted to try out for the Spiro T. Agnew Middle School baseball team, she went into her overprotective turbo-hyper-worrywart mode. I don't understand why. There are far riskier sports than baseball.

She finally agreed to let me try out for baseball, but only if I wore a helmet *at all times*. Not just while at bat or out in the field.

Derp!

Fortunately, Dad stepped in again and talked Mom out of it.

(You know, I bet football is the only sport where Mom would *not* be worried, because in that sport you *do* wear a helmet at all times. Never mind that the whole point of the game is to inflict maximum physical pain on your opponent.)

So I had a green light from the Power Structure. The stage was set. Steve, the ace benchwarmer of the youth leagues, was ready for one of life's major milestones.

The team tryout!

It was only a few days away. But so was the beginning of my dreaded Bean-O-Phobia.

Quick Time-Out about Phobias

You are not born with a phobia. They don't just pop up out of nowhere like a wart.

A phobia grabs hold of your brain only

after you suffer some kind of a traumatic event.

Here's a fairly common example:

Let's say you're wandering barefoot in the Sahara Desert with a Bedouin tribe and you step on a deathstalker scorpion—pretty much the deadliest scorpion on Earth—and it stings you on the big toe and your entire foot swells up like a basketball and agonizing pain shoots through your body like a lightning bolt.

What if that happens? Well, if you survive, it's almost certain that you will develop a crippling fear of deathstalker scorpions.

Scorpion-O-Phobia.

You can also develop a phobia if you merely witness *someone else* suffering a traumatic event.

So if you're wandering in the Sahara Desert with that Bedouin tribe and you see the *chief* get stung by a deathstalker scorpion, and *his* foot swells up like a basketball and agonizing pain shoots through *his* body like a bolt of lightning?

Doesn't matter. You can still develop Scorpion-O-Phobia.

And that's what happened to me. I was a firsthand witness to the infamous Valentine's Day Schnoz Massacre, a gory incident that happened during the Mighty Plumber baseball tryouts.

There was gushing blood! Horrifying screams! A grown man *FAINTED*!!!

Sorry . . .

I'm not ready to tell you about the Valentine's Day Schnoz Massacre yet because—duh. It's a strict rule when writing a book that you build suspense first and don't just spill all the cool gory stuff right off the bat.

So "hang on to your jockstraps," as Coach Earwax likes to say. I'll get to the bloody gore when the suspense builds to the point where you can't stand it any longer.

CHAPTER 2

Dad always tells me, "Ninety percent of success is preparation."

(I have no idea if that number is accurate or if my dad just made it up. But since my dad was once a hotshot athlete, I figure he knows ninety percent more about success than I do.)

In order to be prepared for the baseball tryout, I had to make sure that I had all the right gear. I didn't want to walk out onto the field and suddenly realize I forgot my glove.

I decided to lay my gear out on my bed and make a list, checking stuff off to make sure I had everything I needed.

Before I could do that, I had to deal with Fido, who was wrapped around my ankle and begging for attention.

Quick Time-Out about My Pets

Remember when I told you that I'm an only child? (I hope so, because it was only a few pages ago, so that would be really pathetic if you already forgot.)

Well, there are a few other members of my family: our pets. They're not exactly my brothers or sisters, but they can be just as annoying.

Fido is my pet boa constrictor, in case you didn't figure that out already, and he is very unique. I'll explain why in a minute.

But first there's Frenchy, who is probably the most demented poodle you will ever meet in your entire life, and I'm not even exaggerating. He pretty much lives under my bed and growls and barks at any kind of sound or movement. He only comes out from under the bed when it's absolutely necessary.

I shove Frenchy's food and water dish under the bed, otherwise he might starve or die of thirst and stink up the house like one of those dead rats in the attic.

Then there's Cleo, the duck . . .

. . . who thinks she's a dog.

I bought Cleo when she was a fuzzy duckling with a few bucks I made from selling an NBA player's dirty socks to a sports memorabilia collector.

Except for that whole "thinks she's a dog" thing, Cleo is really smart—smarter than a ninth grader. That's like genius level for a duck and pretty much a major slam to ninth graders.

I also have one of those bug-eyed goldfish who always look like they just cut cheese.

BLOOP!

THAT WASN'T ME!!

I named him Zoner because he has some kind of sleep disorder called narcolepsy that strikes without warning.

Zoner will be cruising around his bowl like a normal bug-eyed goldfish, then suddenly nod off and float belly up. It looks like he's dead, but he's really just sleeping. It's a life-threatening disorder!

But of all our pets, Fido is my favorite. He is by far the coolest pet in the entire world, and I'm not even exaggerating.

Fido and I bonded the day I brought him home from the pet shop. Mom almost blew a head gasket for several reasons: I forgot to get permission from the Power Structure. She is afraid of snakes. And boa constrictors can grow to be ten feet long.

That's big enough to swallow a lunatic poodle.

Fido can even do tricks on command. He can roll over and sit up and stick out his tongue—any trick a dog can do, with a few exceptions.

Even though other people might freak out about having a pet boa constrictor, I'm pretty sure that Fido would never do anything crazy like coil himself around my neck and strangle me until my eyeballs pop out.

But Fido occasionally gets into mischief. One time I left my bedroom door open, and Fido escaped his cage and decided to explore the house. In case you don't know, snakes are very clean creatures. So Fido decided to slither into a bathroom for a warm soak in a bathtub.

Unfortunately, it was the tub in my parents' bathroom.

And Mom was in it.

Okay, so what Mom doesn't understand is that Fido struggles with a major phobia of his own.

Remember those wimpy kids in kindergarten who always threw crying fits and clung to their parents' legs during morning drop-off?

Teachers called it "separation anxiety." Fido has the same fear, but it's not easy to peel a boa constrictor off an ankle. They have the strength of ten kindergarteners!

Which brings me back to my gear checklist. While I was preparing for my baseball tryout, I discovered a major blunder.

CHECKLIST
☑ BASEBALL GLOVE
☑ CLEATS
☑ HAT
☑ SOCKS   NO HAND-ME-DOWNS!!
☑ SUNFLOWER SEEDS
☐ CUP

Derp!

I didn't have an athletic protector.

CHAPTER 3

It might sound crazy, but I was embarrassed to buy a cup. It's a very private piece of athletic gear. I'd rather walk up to a checkout counter and stand in line to buy a tube of hemorrhoid cream. (Not that I'd ever need it!)

I went through my entire youth baseball career without a cup, but I wasn't going to get away with that at Spiro T. Agnew Middle School. Coach Earwax had a strict rule that everyone on the team must wear a cup.

I picked up Fido and stashed him back in the cage, shut the bedroom door, and made an emergency run to O'Callahan's Sporting Goods.

On the way to the store (walking, with no helmet) I met up with my two best friends, Joey Linguini and Carlos Diaz. We're pretty much inseparable.

The three Benchkateers!

Quick Time-Out about My Friends

Sitting the pine is our common bond. Joey, Carlos, and I are benchwarmers who love absolutely everything about sports.

Almost everything.

We live in a sports lover's paradise. There's even a stadium right smack in the middle of our neighborhood. Goodfellow Stadium is where I got those dirty NBA socks that I sold to the memorabilia collector.

BABE'S SOCKS   BABE'S HAT   BABE

BABE RUTH MEMORABILIA

When I ran into Carlos and Joey on the way to the sporting goods store, it was no coincidence. They were waiting for me, and Joey already knew about my decision to try out for the baseball team and my desperate need for a cup.

How did he know? Well, Joey is a psychic, and I'm not even making that up.

He can predict stuff like when a pitcher is going to lose control of a fastball and bean a batter right on the skull. That's a handy thing to know ahead of time, especially if you're the batter.

One time in math class Joey predicted

something during that quiet moment at the beginning of class after the bell but before the teacher starts yakking and scrawling alien symbols on the whiteboard.

A few seconds later the teacher told us to close our books because he was giving us a pop quiz!

Everyone was amazed (and sort of creeped out) except Jimmy Jimerino. He slammed Joey for not predicting the quiz sooner so that he could work up some cheat sheets.

Joey is a small guy, and I'm talking teensy, but he can run faster than any student in our entire school. Maybe even the entire world!

He's like a flea. If you blink, he's gone.

It's a survival skill found in all tiny creatures.

Joey is the quiet middle child in the Linguini family. They have nine really noisy kids, so Joey gets drowned out and forgotten all the time.

Joey really needs to work on raising his voice, though, especially when he has an important prediction to announce.

Carlos is the opposite of Joey. He's slow and loud and sort of overweight, although he calls it "big boned." Carlos is a good guy, but he never stops complaining. He's the biggest grouch at Spiro T. Agnew Middle School.

Carlos gripes about everything, and he hates being a benchwarmer. Carlos believes that he's better at sports than any of the hotshot athletes—including Jimmy Jimerino. He's not, but don't say that to Carlos.

Carlos does have one amazing talent, though. He can burp and speak at the same time. I'm talking entire paragraphs in one belch!

Anyone can belch a single word. It's a cinch.

But Carlos has enough gas bottled up in his gut to burp entire paragraphs.

In youth sports his bodacious belches were morale builders. If our team was getting slaughtered in a game, Carlos would burp-speak in the dugout so loud that even the center fielder could hear it.

If there was such a thing as Major League Burping, Carlos would be a first-round draft choice.

• • •

By the time I met up with Carlos and Joey, they had also decided to try out for the middle school baseball team. That meant we would be going through the rite of passage together. But they needed gear, too.

So the three of us headed off to O'Callahan's Sporting Goods. I needed a cup, and Joey had to buy baseball socks, because he refuses to wear his older brothers' germy hand-me-downs.

Carlos wanted to buy a Frisbee. Why? I don't know. It has nothing to do with baseball, but that's just Carlos.

CHAPTER 4

When we arrived at O'Callahan's Sporting Goods, Becky O'Callahan was at the checkout counter. Becky is the owner's granddaughter.

QUICK TIME-OUT ABOUT BECKY

Everyone at school except Carlos likes Becky. Carlos says he doesn't like her because she's "stuck-up," but the real reason is that he's jealous. Becky is a way better athlete than Carlos.

Becky is definitely not stuck-up. For one thing, she's really good at video games. I heard that she reached Ultimate-Toad level in Bufo Combat, practically the most popular video game in the entire universe, and I'm not even exaggerating.

I've only gotten to Tadpole level, and it took me three months! You can't be stuck-up if you're good at video games, especially Bufo Combat.

Becky also has a great smile. It's not too big and toothy, where you can see way up into her gums. And it's not a tight-lip smile, where you don't see any teeth at all.

Becky has Nature's Near-Perfect Smile. It makes you feel like you're her best friend in the entire universe.

By the way, I really, *really* like Becky, but no one knows. (Er . . . I guess everyone knows NOW since I'm spilling my guts in a book!)

I can't talk to Becky without stuffing my hands in my pants pockets or hooking my thumbs in the belt. It's really awkward. If I don't ditch my hands somewhere, they just sort of flail around in panic looking for a place to hide.

Unfortunately, Becky has a boyfriend—Jimmy Jimerino.

• • •

Jimmy was at the sporting goods store when we arrived. He was leaning on Becky's checkout counter and trying to act all cool in a game-worn NFL football jersey that I sold him last summer for about four times what it's worth.

No way was I going to buy a cup from Becky, especially with Jimmy watching. He'd probably think I was putting the moves on his girlfriend.

I needed someone to buy a cup for me.

Joey couldn't do it because he also has a cup-buying phobia. He uses a hand-me-down cup from one of his older brothers, which makes no sense to me. Joey refuses to wear used baseball socks, but he has no problem wearing a used athletic protector?

Carlos said he'd buy the cup for me, but only if I paid for his Frisbee.

What a buddy. I would've told Carlos to shove a Frisbee up his left nostril, but I was stuck. I needed his help.

Joey and Carlos went to pick out their stuff. Joey was done in about five seconds. He took his new socks up to the checkout counter and stood there waiting.

JOCKS? ROCKS? BLOCKS?...HELLO! ANYONE THERE??

SOCKS.

Meanwhile, Carlos had to examine every single Frisbee in the entire store, as if one Frisbee wasn't exactly as round as all the others.

I killed time in the baseball section. The store had official Major League baseballs on display. They were fresh out of the box and carefully stacked up in the shape of a pyramid. It must have taken someone an entire week to build.

I wanted to buy a new baseball, but I didn't have enough money because I gave every cent I had to Carlos for my athletic protector and his stupid Frisbee.

While I was admiring the pyramid, a toddler who was about the size of Joey wandered over.

A pyramid made of baseballs is a huge temptation for a toddler.

OFFICIAL MLB BASEBALLS

MINE!!

He tried to grab one of the baseballs—one at the very bottom of the pyramid.

I knew THAT wasn't going to end well, so I stopped him. Then I reached up and grabbed the baseball at the very top of the pyramid. But when I turned to give it to the little tyke, my elbow bumped a baseball on the bottom row.

Avalanche!

The pyramid that probably took someone an entire week to build was ruined. I had about two seconds to act. Naturally, I chose to do what any intelligent person would do in that situation.

I bolted.

I ducked behind a hockey display and left the rug rat to take the blame. Then he started to cry, and my conscience got to me.

I was just about to come out of hiding when Becky rushed over. She wasn't upset about the collapsed pyramid, though. She was worried about the rug rat. Becky picked him up and gave him a hug and told him everything was okay.

And then she gave him a brand-new base-ball—for free!

You see? That's why everyone at Spiro T. Agnew Middle School except Carlos likes Becky O'Callahan.

Carlos finally stopped fooling around and chose a Frisbee. (A round one!) He paid for the Frisbee and my cup and then joined me and Joey outside.

Carlos handed me the athletic protector, and I looked at the box.

Derp!

I tried to get Carlos to exchange it for a smaller size, but he was busy planning his future on the Professional Frisbee Tour.

I went home and tried on the XXL cup.

Fortunately, my dad bailed me out. I showed him my cup problem, and when he was finally done with his laughing fit, Dad drove to O'Callahan's and bought me the right size.

CHAPTER 5

Now that I had all my gear together, the next step in preparing for the tryout was to practice my skills. In case you don't know, in between seasons the human body can actually forget how to throw a baseball and swing a bat.

I really wanted to at least toss the ball around, but I needed a second person, because it's practically impossible to play catch with yourself.

Dad had to leave on a business trip, so I asked my friends.

Joey couldn't play catch because he had chores to do at home. The middle child in a large family always gets stuck with unpleasant chores that none of the other kids will do.

I asked Carlos to play catch, but he reminded me that he's a natural athlete, so he had no need to practice for the baseball tryout. You can probably guess I had some serious doubts about that statement.

I was on my own.

O'Callahan's Sporting Goods sells those fancy Toss-O-Matic gizmos that bounce balls right back at you. It's *almost* like playing catch with yourself.

One time Carlos tried the store display Toss-O-Matic. The baseball rebounded faster than he expected and conked him in the forehead. (So much for his "natural athlete" claim.) For two days, Carlos had a huge bump on his forehead.

I wasn't real motivated to buy a Toss-O-Matic and grow a nose on my forehead. And I didn't want to go through the checkout line at O'Callahan's Sporting Goods. Becky would think I was a loser with no friends who would play catch with me.

I decided to improvise and throw a baseball against the fence in my backyard, then field the rebound as a grounder.

It worked pretty well—except when the ball would hit a gap between fence boards and ricochet sideways across my backyard.

BARK!
BARK!
BARK!
YELP!!

I was just starting to get my arm warmed up when my next-door neighbor called the police. Mrs. Smoot is a pet hoarder with about ten million cats, by my estimate. No one in the neighborhood even knows what she looks like, because Mrs. Smoot never leaves the house.

When the ball started banging against the fence, Mrs. Smoot's stupid cats freaked out.

I guess they thought a cat-eating Rottweiler was trying to break through the fence with a sledgehammer.

A police officer showed up at my house.

He was sympathetic about my need to practice for the baseball tryout, but he told me to quit throwing the ball against the fence.

At that point I pretty much gave up on getting any practice in before the baseball tryout. I decided to just show up cold and wing it.

Big mistake.

CHAPTER 6

The Mighty Plumbers baseball tryout was held after school on Valentine's Day.

We all gathered in center field. Our coach climbed up into the bleachers to address us.

He was holding a clipboard, which is a coach's most valuable possession. It contains top-secret notes about all the players.

Clipboards also contain important wisdom that a coach needs to build a winning team.

[WHEN TALKING TO PLAYERS, ALWAYS STAND IN HEROIC POSE ON TOP ROW OF CENTER-FIELD BLEACHERS.]

Coach Earwax blew his whistle to start tryouts and yelled, "Listen up!"

Every coach in the entire world yells "Listen up!" It gets instant attention, like when a beach lifeguard yells "Shark!"

We all instantly stopped yakking and squirming—except Joey. He's kind of a fidgety guy, which is another survival skill found in most tiny creatures.

But Joey had good reason to squirm. He forgot the first step in preparing for the team tryout.

DERP! FORGOT MY GLOVE!!

I blinked and Joey was gone.

Coach Earwax told us that only fifteen players would make the team. Everyone except Jimmy Jimerino did a quick count. He wasn't worried, because hotshot athletes never get cut.

There were thirty of us (counting Joey) trying out for the team. That meant that by the end of tryouts, half of us would be hiding in restroom stalls without food for a week because of the shame.

We looked around, trying to act all nonchalant and cool while we sized up the competition. Right away I spotted one kid who probably wouldn't make the cut.

Ricky Schnauzer was wearing khakis, a collared shirt, and hard-sole shoes! And it was pretty easy to tell that his glove was brand-spanking-new because there was an O'Callahan's Sporting Goods price tag still attached to the webbing.

Street clothes, hard-sole shoes, and a spanking-new glove! Ricky Schnauzer was toast.

Joey returned with his glove. He had only been gone about thirty seconds—and his house is six blocks away! Then Joey had another one of his psychic episodes.

GIRL.

PEARL?

CURL?

HURL?

WHAAA?

Joey didn't speak up, as usual, so we were all confused until about ten seconds later, when Vinny Pascual started gagging as if he'd just swallowed gum down the wrong pipe, which is exactly what had happened. It looked like Vinny was going to blow chunks, so I figured Joey had said "Hurl." But that wasn't the prediction.

Vinny was choking on his gum because he was startled by the sight of a girl running toward us wearing metal cleats and carrying a baseball glove.

Becky O'Callahan was trying out for the baseball team!

Everyone was shocked—including Jimmy Jimerino. Apparently Becky had told no one that she was trying out for the team, not even her hotshot athlete boyfriend.

We were all dead silent—except for Vinny.

Carlos gave him a hard slap on the back, and the gum wad shot out of Vinny's mouth and lodged in Skinny Dennis's hair.

Coach Earwax was caught off guard by Becky. It's totally okay for girls to try out for the school baseball team, but it had never happened in the history of Spiro T. Agnew Middle School.

Coach Earwax scribbled a top-secret note on his clipboard and mumbled his way through a "review" of baseball fundamentals that everyone should have learned back in Pee Wee league. Then he told us to run out and stand at the positions we wanted to play.

That started a mad dash to the most popular positions, like pitcher, shortstop, and first base.

One kid got so disoriented in all the excitement that he ran off the field and disappeared.

One less competitor!

Shortstop is a baseball position reserved for hotshot athletes, so naturally Carlos chose that position, along with two other fools who didn't realize that Jimmy Jimerino already owned first-string shortstop.

Becky ran to the pitcher's mound and lined up behind three guys.

Joey zipped out to second base because it's practically a rule in baseball that tiny guys play second base.

I jogged out to right field. No one in their

right mind actually *chooses* to play right field, but it was a strategic move. If I was the only one trying out for that position, then I'd definitely make the team.

Unfortunately, I had company. Skinny Dennis and Dewey Taylor somehow had figured out the same strategy.

CHAPTER 7

In case you've never been in a baseball try-out, the pace is really quick.

Fielding—Badda-boom!

Hitting—Badda-bing!

Coach Earwax started hitting grounders to the infield.

Jimmy was awesome, of course. Every time he fielded a grounder and made a perfect throw to first base, Coach Earwax would get all gushy.

"Atta babe" is like "Listen up." It's another term that coaches use all the time. "Atta babe" means a player did something that will get a player picked for the team.

After every spectacular play, Jimmy had to immediately look over at Becky to see if she was watching. She wasn't. Becky kept her attention on the coach, which is exactly what you're supposed to do instead of gushing over a hotshot athlete.

Meanwhile, Carlos made a huge error in judgment.

Coach Earwax actually stopped practice and reminded Carlos that he was no longer playing youth baseball, so he'd better knock off the "baby stuff."

Ouch.

I'm not sure if it was the pressure of trying out or the fact that Becky, the prettiest girl in school, was standing on the pitcher's mound, but players were dropping balls, muffing grounders, and making bad throws.

At one point Coach Earwax told Vinny Pascual to "keep your head down" when fielding grounders so the ball wouldn't roll under his glove.

Vinny took Coach a little too literally, and boy did he pay the price.

The ball knocked out two of Vinny's front teeth. He looked like an Ultimate Fighter dude who got karate kicked in the mouth. It was awesome.

Vinny picked up his two teeth out of the dirt and ran home. Another player gone.

Carlos continued to struggle. After his embarrassing "baby stuff" disaster, he missed three easy grounders. Each time he flubbed the play, Carlos would scowl at his glove as if *it* was the problem!

Joey did pretty well at second base. He's so fast, nothing got past him. But Joey's arm is really tiny, so his throws landed halfway to first base and then rolled the rest of the way.

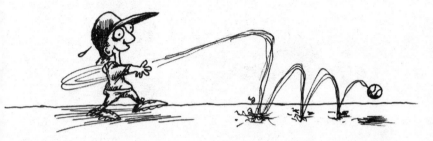

Coach hit three hard grounders to Becky on the mound. She scooped up the balls like a pro and made perfect throws to first base. Coach looked pleasantly surprised. He didn't say "Atta babe," but he jotted a top-secret note on his clipboard.

Then it was the outfielders' turn to field hits. I was the first victim. Unfortunately, I was distracted.

A few feet away, a gopher had poked his head out of a hole and glared at me. I was pretty sure it was challenging me to a contest.

The gopher won only because my eyeballs dried out.

I didn't want to be distracted by a rodent and blow the tryout, so I tried to scare it back into its hole.

I took off my glove and chucked it at the gopher . . .

. . . just as Coach Earwax yelled, "Right fielder! Heads up!"

He hit a high fly ball to me. I had only one choice.

In case you're wondering, catching a high fly ball with your bare hands hurts. A lot.

But that wasn't even the worst part of the gopher fiasco. Remember when I told you that between seasons the human body can forget things, such as how to throw a baseball? Well, my arm was struck with total amnesia.

I threw the ball as hard as I could toward home plate, but it sailed way off course over the fence and into the faculty parking lot.

The ball ricocheted back and forth and set off about a dozen car alarms.

Ms. Vielhaber, my English teacher, was walking to her car, and the loud racket scared her so badly she screamed like someone in a horror movie and dove underneath the groundskeeper's filthy pickup truck.

I slunk back behind the other two guys trying out for right field and tried to make myself invisible. If I could have fit, I would have crawled into the gopher hole.

Coach Earwax scribbled something on his clipboard, and I'm pretty sure it wasn't "strong arm."

I figured my performance in the fielding drills didn't exactly fry Coach's burger. I had one more chance to show him what I could do.

CHAPTER 8

Coach took the mound to pitch to us. We all got ten swings, and on the last pitch we were supposed to bunt the ball and run to first base as if our lives depended on it.

Jimmy Jimerino got a hit on every one of his pitches, including a blast over the center-field fence. He looked at Becky and arched his eyebrow as if to say, "That one was for YOU!"

Coach Earwax and all of Jimmy's posse

gave him "Atta babes," but Skinny Dennis *really* sucked up.

Bombdiggity? I hadn't heard anyone use that word since preschool.

After his home run blast, Jimmy bunted and ran to first base. He would have been thrown out, but he plowed into the first baseman like a linebacker sacking a quarterback.

Ronnie Howard, the first baseman, got knocked on his butt and dropped the ball. He wasn't hurt, but Ronnie is kind of a drama king. He blubbered and moaned and milked the scene a little *too* much.

I don't think he was expecting that Coach would send him home "out of an abundance of caution."

Another player gone!

Becky was outstanding at bat. Five clean hits in ten pitches. And when she bunted, Becky beat out the throw to first base by a mile.

Carlos got up to bat and fouled off all his pitches *and* the bunt. But one of his fouls was a monster fly ball that flew out of the ballpark and bounced down Seventh Street toward the stadium.

Carlos looked surprised at first. Then he snapped out of it and got all cocky. As if he hits it that far *all* the time.

Everyone except Jimmy was impressed. Coach Earwax even scribbled a top-secret note on his clipboard. Carlos probably figured it was something complimentary about his long foul ball.

Joey's batting went as you might expect. Coach Earwax had a hard time getting the pitch into his strike zone.

Whenever a pitch did manage to get close, Joey would hit a slow grounder to shortstop. Jimmy fielded the grounders behind his back, between legs, with eyes closed. Showing off for Becky.

Joey rocked the bunt, though. It dribbled only a couple of feet in front of the plate, but by the time the catcher picked up the ball, Joey was standing on third base!

Coach Earwax quickly scribbled another top-secret note on his clipboard. A speedy player with a tiny strike zone might come in handy.

When it was my turn to hit, I tried to impress Coach with my batting stance. I copied it from a former major league baseball player named Julio Franco.

Quick Time-Out about Julio Franco

Julio always stood with his knees knocked together, arms up and the bat straight over his head with the barrel pointed right at the pitcher like a cannon. Then he waggled the end of the bat to purposely mess with the pitcher's brain. (I'm not even making this up. You can Google Julio Franco.)

At home in front of the mirror, I had fiddled with Julio's stance and came up with my own version.

I named it the Mind-Bender.

• • •

When I got to the plate, I went right into my Mind-Bender stance. Coach Earwax was caught off guard. He had a look on his face like he'd just smelled a dirty diaper and stared at me like that stupid gopher.

So I stared back.

Finally, Coach blinked and threw a pitch that bounced three feet in front of the plate.

It worked! Coach's brain was messed up by the Mind-Bender. Unfortunately, so was my body.

He got the next nine pitches across the plate, but the crazy batting stance was hard to unwind. I swung and missed every single pitch.

On my last swing I managed to nick the ball—barely. It dropped onto the dirt next to me like a spilled snow cone.

Coach said I got a piece of it, but I think he was being sarcastic.

Fortunately, I pulled off a really good bunt that dribbled down the third-base line.

Becky hustled over and fielded the bunt

because Ricky Schnauzer was playing third base and he was, er, preoccupied.

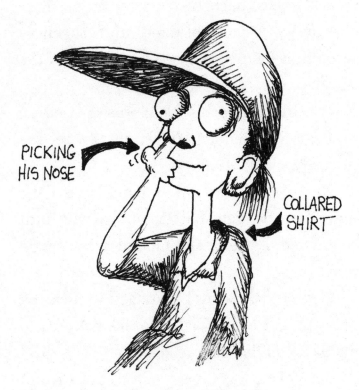

PICKING HIS NOSE

COLLARED SHIRT

I almost beat Becky's throw to first, though. I think that made a good impression, because as I jogged off the field, Coach Earwax yelled, "Atta babe!"

Or maybe he was talking to Becky.

The last batter up was Dewey Taylor, one of the other players trying out for my position in right field.

Dewey is kind of a picky guy, and he didn't like the first few pitches that Coach threw. Too slow. Too low. Too far outside.

Joey was standing right behind me, and I heard him say something spooky. It turned out to be the most famous psychic-Joey prediction of all time.

SCHNOZ.

Coach Earwax overcorrected on the next pitch to Dewey. He reared back and tossed a fastball that was high and inside.

Poor Dewey. He was like the bad guy in a Western movie who gets plugged by the sheriff before he can even draw the gun out of his holster.

The ball hit Dewey right smack on the nose. It sounded just like my baseball hitting Mrs. Smoot's fence. Dewey was knocked flat on his back. Blood gushed out of both nostrils and soaked the front of his T-shirt.

His nose was smashed sideways on his face!

Everyone on the ball field was stunned and silent, except Skinny Dennis, who screamed like someone in a horror movie.

Mr. Joseph, the school groundskeeper,

looked up from raking the grass behind the dugout, and when he saw all the bloody gore, he keeled over backward and fainted!

I was standing in front of the dugout. I wanted to run over and help Dewey, but my feet wouldn't budge.

Coach Earwax and Becky immediately ran to home plate. Coach tore off Dewey's T-shirt that probably cost a lot of money and used it to stop the bleeding while Becky held Dewey's head in her lap.

Jimmy Jimerino ran to the dugout to get his cell phone, but he wasn't going to call for help.

Fortunately, Becky gave Jimmy the stink eye, and he changed his mind.

After Mr. Joseph recovered from fainting, he drove Dewey to the doctor in his filthy pickup truck. As they pulled away, we all knew Dewey was going to be okay, because he stuck an arm out the window and gave us a thumbs-up.

Dewey's gory broken-nose incident would soon become known in Spiro T. Agnew Middle School folklore as the "Valentine's Day Schnoz Massacre."

Later that night, after all the drama during the tryout, it took me three hours to get to sleep. Part of the reason was that Frenchy was under my bed snoring like a dragon. But mostly I kept picturing poor Dewey with his nose bent sideways and blood all over his T-shirt.

When I finally did fall asleep, I had a horrible nightmare.

My brain was in the grip of an epic fear.

Bean-O-Phobia!

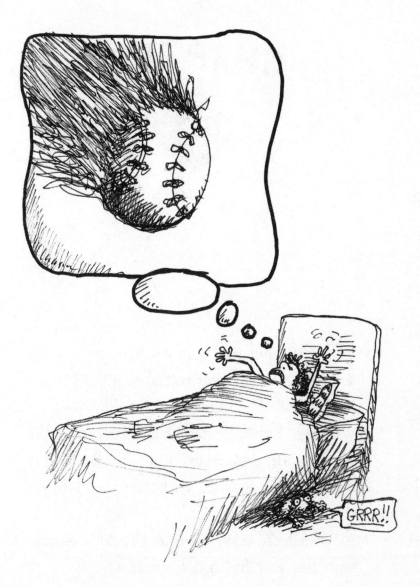

GRRR!!

CHAPTER 9

The next morning before school, my friends and I hustled over to the ball field to see if we'd made the team.

Coach Earwax tacked the roster to the dugout wall, then ducked out in a big hurry to avoid eye contact with the poor shlubs who'd been cut.

We all crowded around the list. Jimmy Jimerino and his posse made the team, of course. They slapped hands and bumped chests, then they left to show off their sweat stains to girls.

It was easy to tell the players who got cut. They all wandered off like zombies. Ricky Schnauzer was one of them.

Becky made the team. She flashed Nature's Near-Perfect Smile and made a pumping gesture with her fist. As Becky walked past, she gave me a wink! My knees wobbled, and I'm not even exaggerating.

Finally, the moment of truth. The major milestone. Success or painful rejection.

I looked at the roster. Dewey Taylor's name was at the top of the list, even though he didn't complete the tryout. Dewey wasn't there to see it, but I thought this was a really nice gesture by Coach Earwax.

At the very bottom of the list was scribbled—not typed like the rest of the names—"Joey Linguini, Carlos Diaz, Steve Moore," in that order. We apparently made it by the skin of our teeth.

Carlos grumbled because Joey's name was above his, but we all slapped hands and bumped chests just like the hotshot athletes.

We didn't stink!

As we walked off the field, I looked over at home plate. Mr. Joseph had raked clean the bloody spot where Dewey Taylor got beaned right in the schnoz.

But in my mind I saw Dewey's bloody sideways nose.

And a baseball the size of a meteor.

CHAPTER 10

I wasn't the only one who couldn't stop thinking about what was already being called the St. Valentine's Day Schnoz Massacre. Everyone at school was talking about Dewey.

Everyone except Jimmy Jimerino.

Crazy rumors were flying all over the place.

That last one was my personal favorite.

The rumors came to a screeching halt, though, when Dewey was dropped off in front of school.

We all saw the true damage: both of Dewey's eyes were swollen and bruised. He was wearing a masklike bandage that made him look like the villain in a horror movie who causes people to scream.

No one screamed, though. Dewey got the celebrity treatment. Everyone crowded around and slapped him on the back and gave him high fives. Becky gave him a big hug—right in front of Jimmy.

But Dewey told us he was done with baseball. He would play no more. Forever. He was going to do track and field instead, because the chances of getting beaned on the nose by a baseball while running are pretty slim.

I was just about to ask Dewey if he had nightmares about baseballs the size of meteors, but it was time to head into school.

Quick Time-Out about My School

Spiro T. Agnew is not your normal middle school.

First of all, you probably noticed that the

name is kind of odd. Most schools are named after presidents or poets or military heroes or other famous dead people. Not my school.

Our dead guy was a mere *vice* president who resigned from office for being corrupt. Miss Dubois, my history teacher, said it happened a long time ago. She is older than the internet, but her mind is still sharp enough to remember the entire episode.

When someone asks us where we go to school, all the students except the kiss-ups answer "Spiro." It's a lot quicker to say, and you don't have to explain all that corrupt-politician thing.

The second you walk in the front doorway, you notice something eerie. Our school is really quiet.

We don't even have a bell that rings when class begins and ends. We have a recorded "jingle." It sounds like one of those dangling wind chimes that people hang in their backyards to calm their nerves.

Our hallways don't have linoleum or tile floors. We have carpeting that muffles all the ruckus when students rush to the next class.

The only sound you hear is soft music that's piped into every hallway in the entire school. But it's not the kind of music you actually want to hear. If you've ever been in a dentist's office, you know what I mean.

At Spiro there is a strict rule: no raising your voice in the carpeted hallways. We're forced to communicate in whispers.

How is that even possible?

Ms. Theresa is the person responsible for turning Spiro into a dentist's office. She's our school principal. We call her Mother T., and I am only slightly exaggerating when I say that she is probably 120 years old.

I'm always thinking that she might crumble into a pile of bones at any moment.

Mother T. patrols the hallways, smiling, with her hands folded as if she's praying for world peace. She looks like the saintliest person in the entire world.

Trickery!

Mother T. is the strictest school principal you could possibly imagine. She rules Spiro with a mysterious mental power, sort of like that old dude in the Star Wars movies who could turn a guy into a puppet with just a few words.

Mother T.'s evil goodness is everywhere at Spiro.

For example, all our restrooms are sparkling clean and odor free, and I'm not even making that up. No overflowing trash cans. No sinks with green scum. No graffiti.

When students from normal schools visit Spiro and borrow our clean and odor-free facilities, they always walk out with a freaky look on their face.

IT'S SO CLEAN!!

It's embarrassing!

• • •

Later in the day, after Dewey returned to school with his face in a horror movie villain mask, I was in one of Spiro's clean and odor-free restrooms when I got a chance to ask Dewey about the Valentine's Day Schnoz Massacre.

I was in front of the mirror trying to flatten a rebellious clump of hair on the back of my head that stuck up like a twig and refused to blend in with the crowd.

Dewey walked in and went right to the mirror. I think he wanted to make sure his nose hadn't flopped back over to the side of his face.

I smashed down the rebellious clump of hair so it wouldn't be a distraction, then I asked Dewey if getting hit on the nose by a baseball is more painful than, say, getting kicked in the shin, which is one of the most sensitive bones in the entire human body.

Yeah, it was a dumb question, but I needed to know where Dewey's injury ranked on the Pain Meter. I figured if it didn't hurt worse than a kick to the shin, then maybe I wouldn't be afraid of the ball next time I went up to bat.

Dewey stopped fiddling with his mask. He turned and stared at me with his swollen and bruised eyes.

Dewey slowly nodded his head yes.

I was doomed.

CHAPTER

A t the first baseball practice of the season, everyone was excited because we all had made the cut. We all had made the team. We all were . . .

MIGHTY PLUMBERS

But there was another hurdle. We all were competing in practice to see who would be playing in the games and who would be sitting on the bench.

Carlos said he was "one hundred and ten percent certain" that he would be the first-string shortstop. I was one hundred and ten percent certain that Carlos would be sitting the pine and grouching for the entire season. I didn't even need a crystal ball.

But I did ask Joey to do his psychic thing and foretell whether he and I would be starters or benchwarmers. Joey wasn't in the mood, though. He apparently can't just turn his power on and off like a lightbulb.

Coach Earwax climbed to the top of the center-field bleachers and got into his heroic pose.

TAKE A LAP!!

That is without a doubt one of the most annoying coaching commands in all of sports—right up there with "Drop and give me a hundred push-ups!"

We had to run a lap all the way around the outside of the baseball field. And we couldn't just jog. Everyone had to run as fast as humanly possible in order to work our bodies into finely tuned athletic machines.

If Coach caught even one player "doggin' it," the entire team would have to run another lap.

Joey completed the lap in about five seconds. I was in the middle of the pack. But good ol' natural-athlete Carlos jogged around the field and came in *way* behind the rest of the team.

I don't think Carlos was doggin' it on purpose. He's just a big-boned guy, and that extra weight can really slow you down.

The entire team had to take another lap because of Carlos, and he got the major stink eye from Jimmy Jimerino and his posse.

Carlos ran the next lap even *slower* because he was still out of breath from the first lap.

Thankfully, Coach Earwax didn't make us run another one, because I think he realized that Carlos would only get slower with every lap.

Coach Earwax moved to home plate and began hitting balls to players at every position. He told the infielders to scoop up ground balls and throw to first base. Outfielders were to catch fly balls and throw to second base.

Since Dewey Taylor was retired from the

game of baseball, the only two players competing for starting right fielder were myself and Skinny Dennis.

Skinny is probably the least hotshot of the hotshot athletes in Jimmy Jimerino's posse, but I was still facing pretty stiff competition.

When it was our turn to field fly balls, I went first. Skinny probably would have insisted on going first, but he was distracted.

Coach Earwax hit a short blooper to right field, and I had to beat cheeks to make the catch before it dropped. I made one of those cool "shoestring" catches where you nab the ball on the run with the glove just inches above your foot.

It was awesome. No brag. It's just a fact.

Unfortunately, I was so excited about catching the ball that I forgot where to throw it. First base? Second base?

Don't ask me why, because I can't explain a brain wreck, but I cocked my arm and threw the ball halfway *between* first and second bases.

Derp!

There was no one there to catch my throw, of course. The first baseman was standing at first base, and the second baseman was standing at second base.

My throw landed in the deserted stretch of dirt between the bases and rolled into the infield grass.

Brilliant.

Jimmy Jimerino retrieved the ball and he yelled, "Atta babe, Steve!"

I probably should have given Jimmy the benefit of the doubt, but I'm pretty sure he was being sarcastic.

When Skinny Dennis took his turn as right fielder—after losing his staring contest with the rodent—he caught an easy fly ball and threw it to second base just as Coach Earwax had instructed.

The rest of the fielding drills went well, which means I didn't suffer any more brain wrecks. I caught every ball and threw it to the correct base. But I had a feeling that Skinny was in the lead for first-string right fielder.

CHAPTER

My ranking didn't improve during batting practice. In fact, it hit rock bottom. Bean-O-Phobia reared its ugly head.

Coach Earwax did not pitch for batting practice. He probably had developed a phobia of his own the day before. Like, er, maybe a morbid fear of clobbering a player right in the schnoz with a baseball.

Instead, he put Jimmy Jimerino in at pitcher, which was the worst thing that could

have happened to someone who was struggling to make first string.

Quick Time-Out about Jimmy Jimerino

Jimmy insists on playing only shortstop in games, but he is by far the best pitcher his age in the entire city. Maybe even the world.

His fastballs make scary hissing sounds on their way to the plate. They're freaky fast, like Joey. If you blink, the ball is already in the catcher's mitt.

And Jimmy's curveballs are practically impossible to hit. They come in right at your head, and at the last instant they loop down and right over the plate. As Coach Earwax says, they fake you right out of your jock!

● ● ●

No one on the team got many hits off Jimmy during batting practice. Even Becky had a hard time. She took ten swings and only got one hit. But it was an epic hit—a screaming line drive right back at the pitcher's mound.

KA-BOOM!!

Everyone on the team except Jimmy's kiss-up posse yelled, "Atta babe, Becky!"

I was the last player to hit in batting practice. On the way to the plate, I tried not to think about Dewey Taylor and the bloody gore, but Bean-O-Phobia had grabbed hold of my brain.

While Jimmy was waiting for me to step into the batter's box, I stalled by going through a series of useless motions that I learned from watching major league baseball players:

... SPIT ON GROUND,
ADJUST CUP...
SCRATCH BUTT...

SCRITCH!
SCRITCH!

Coach Earwax finally ran out of patience and yelled, "Batter up!"

I stepped into the batter's box and twisted my body into the Mind-Bender batting stance. I pointed the end of my bat at Jimmy and wiggled it to mess with his weak and useless brain.

It didn't work out.

Jimmy just grinned and started into his windup. I swallowed hard, and my legs started shaking. Then my hips. Then my arms.

My entire body was shaking!

Jimmy threw the pitch. The baseball streaked toward the plate. It seemed to get bigger. And bigger. And BIGGER.

It was my nightmare!

I dove out of the batter's box. At the last instant, the ball looped down and right over the plate. Curveball. A perfect strike.

And I was facedown in the dirt.

I stood up and spit dirt out of my mouth. The entire team was laughing—even Joey and Carlos, although they were trying to hide it behind their gloves.

I looked over at Coach Earwax. He was pinching the bridge of his nose with his thumb and forefinger. His face was all scrunched up as if he was in horrible pain.

At least he wasn't laughing.

I retrieved my helmet, which had flown off and landed next to the dugout. My bat was lying next to third base.

I felt like running off the field, sprinting down Seventh Street, and never coming back, but Coach Earwax ordered me to get back up to the plate.

Ouch.

Jimmy Jimerino was waiting for me, smiling like a cat who was toying with a mouse.

All his pitches were right over the plate. Fastballs. Curveballs. Sliders. Even a knuckleball!

Each time, I ducked or flinched or closed my eyes and covered my head. I swung the bat only once, but the ball was already in the catcher's mitt.

Derp!

Finally, Coach Earwax had seen enough and told the entire team to run *ten* laps.

I got the major stink eye from everyone on the team except Joey, Carlos, and Becky.

CHAPTER 13

My descent into the pit of Bean-O-Phobia had begun.

In every batting practice, I tried my hardest to hit the ball. But I either dove into the dirt or swung and whiffed.

The fear of getting beaned in the schnoz had scrambled my brain and bamboozled my body.

Skinny Dennis was chosen to be the starter in right field, and I took my position on the bench.

We started playing league games, but I didn't get to the plate very often. I was right back to the role I'd played in the youth leagues. Coach Earwax only put me in when it was garbage time and the score was about a hundred to zip.

And whenever I did get to bat, my phobia kicked in with humiliating results. Let me walk you through a few of the, er, highlights.

In our first game of the season against the A. E. Neuman Middle School Madmen, I got up to bat in the last inning. Bean-O-Phobia kicked in, and I slunk as far back in the batter's box as possible to keep from getting hit. Then I swung at the ball like a lunatic.

Three pitches, three whiffs.

In our game against the Fighting Fur Balls of T. S. Eliot Academy, I got another chance at bat. The image of a baseball the size of a meteor flashed before my eyes, and my entire body froze. I couldn't move a finger. I was like that gopher—I didn't even blink!

THE GAME ENDED AN HOUR AGO. YOU SHOULD GO HOME.

Brilliant.

And when we played Our Lady of Perpetual Help, Bean-O-Phobia totally possessed my body. In a panic, I threw my bat at the ball as it crossed the plate. Miraculously, it made contact.

The bat skidded all the way down the first-base line, and the ball ricocheted into the umpire's face mask.

Derp!

I got kicked out of the game for purposely throwing my bat.

At the next practice Coach Earwax told everyone to run *twenty* laps because "Mighty Plumbers do not throw baseball bats."

I got the worst group stink eye in the entire history of baseball.

After those humiliating incidents, my reputation spread throughout the league. I was a marked man.

Even at school there was no escaping the shame of Bean-O-Phobia. It was as if I had some kind of hideous disease. I couldn't walk

the carpeted hallways of Spiro without sens-
ing that every whisper was all about me.

Or maybe it was just my imagination.

CHAPTER

On the day of our last regular-season game, I just wanted to hide in a toilet stall instead of going to class. And I especially dreaded walking into Gossip Central.

The cafeteria.

Quick Time-Out about the Cafeteria

A middle school cafeteria is the last place you want to go if you have a humiliating phobia.

It is a major gossip zone. The entire student body is crammed into one place. There's nothing to do there except stuff your face with crummy food and yak about other students.

Our cafeteria is the only place at Spiro that is just like every other middle school. We even have linoleum floors!

Mother T. once tried carpeting in the cafeteria. The day after the carpet was installed, the lunch menu featured spaghetti and meatballs. You can probably guess how that worked out. They yanked the stained carpet and put in linoleum the very next day.

Our cafeteria walls are plastered with all kinds of goofy school spirit slogans.

Oh, yeah. Our school color is teal.

Teal is sort of a sickly green, like what you'd get if you mixed brussels sprouts and milk in a blender. I am not even going to show that color to you because you might blow chunks.

Joey, Carlos, and I always sit at the same corner table in the back of the cafeteria. It's an excellent location, because we have a great view of the entire room.

You can't just walk into the Spiro cafeteria and sit anywhere. You *can*, but you'd be taking a huge chance, because every table is pretty much "claimed" by a certain social group. If you choose the wrong table, it would be awkward.

My friends and I call our table "C Central." That's because our cumulative GPA is just about a C average, which also happens to match our average athletic ability.

The C Central table isn't exclusive, though. We welcome anyone. The table's cumulative GPA can rise or fall depending on who joins us for lunch. So if Jessica Whitehead, the school genius, ever sat with us, our table GPA would instantly shoot up.

And if Jimmy Jimerino ever sat down with us, the table's athletic ranking would skyrocket.

Never gonna happen, though.

Jimmy sits at the head of the Jock Table. He's like a king presiding over the daily feast. All the chairs at the Jock Table are assigned to Jimmy's kiss-up posse, who laugh their buns off at all his lame jokes.

Here's one of Jimmy's nuggets:

Jimmy tells that same joke about twice a week, but it's a rule at the Jock Table that you have to laugh your buns off even though you've heard the same joke a billion times.

• • •

On the day of the last regular-season game, Jimmy and his entourage walked by C Central table on their way to the Jock Table.

Jimmy greeted our table with his pet nicknames for us. The nickname he gave

Joey was sort of a slam, although I think Joey's psychic mind was on something horrible looming in the future.

His nickname for Carlos is a real zinger: "Belch Boy." Thinking up that one probably drained Jimmy's entire pool of imagination.

For a long time Jimmy couldn't think of a nickname for me. He would look at me and try to think of one, then give up. I think it's because there wasn't anything about me that stuck out as nickname material.

(That's an advantage to being average, by the way. You don't attract attention. I would probably be a really good international spy, because I blend right in with the crowd.)

But that day Jimmy finally came up with my nickname.

At baseball practice the day before, Coach Earwax announced that I was a candidate for "Goose Egg." It is a "trophy" awarded to any player who finishes the entire season with a batting average of, er, ZERO.

No one in the history of Spiro T. Agnew Middle School had ever been Goosed.

Jimmy walked by our table and announced my nickname to the entire cafeteria.

Brilliant.

CHAPTER 15

The Mighty Plumbers' last regular-season game was against a team at the very bottom of the league standings, which was appropriate, because my struggle with Bean-O-Phobia was about to hit an all-time low.

It was an away game against Nike Preparatory Academy, the newest member of our league. Not much was known about the private school except that it had superb academics, vast wealth, and crummy athletics.

In youth baseball an away game just means that you move from the third-base dugout to the first-base dugout, because all the teams play on the same fields.

Big deal.

In middle school you actually travel to a baseball field at a school in a different part of the city. Away games are a blast. It's like a field trip: bus ride, snack bags, and—best of all—early dismissal from school!

Coach Earwax had the team gather in front of school. We were all decked out in our mighty teal-colored uniforms. I could see students watching us out the windows from their final-period classrooms. They all had glum looks on their faces as if they regretted not trying out for the baseball team.

The bus pulled up. As we filed on board, Miss Ekolie, the cafeteria manager, handed out our snack bags. Carlos always thinks about his stomach, so he was all excited.

Until he looked inside.

SNACK BAG

CELERY

CHIA SEEDS

CARROTS

BRUSSELS SPROUTS

TOFU

Brussels sprouts!

I knew Mother T. had to be responsible for *that* dirty trick. How did she expect us to

perform at a peak athletic level on the baseball field with vegetables in our stomachs?

Fortunately, we had been warned by
Becky's older brother not to count on the
road trip snack bags. Everyone on the team
had loaded their gear bags with bubble gum
and sunflower seeds—all the essentials for
peak athletic performance.

My friends and I got on the bus and immediately tried to get the best seats.

At the very back of the bus you can pull
all kinds of pranks without getting in trouble
with the coach or distracting the bus driver.

It's always good to have some kind of activity planned to help kill time on a road trip. I was thinking about starting a vegetable food fight. Carlos claimed he was going to moon a pedestrian, but I think it was all talk.

Joey wanted to play a road game called Perdiddle, where you get points for spotting cars with one burned-out headlight. We had to point out to Joey that it was still broad daylight.

Unfortunately, our plans for the back row were ruined by Jimmy Jimerino and his jock posse.

Joey, Carlos, and I were stuck with the *worst* seats on the bus.

The front row.

Carlos and I sat in the two seats right behind the driver. Joey sat across the aisle in the seat with Coach Earwax.

Joey got the worst of it. Apparently Coach's bad habit with the car key and the earwax is only a habit for the dugout. On road trips Coach Earwax yanks out nose hairs with his fingers!

The highlight of the trip happened after Joey did his psychic thing.

About ten seconds later the bus hit a huge rut in the road. The jolt caused Coach Earwax to sock himself in the schnoz, and it started bleeding.

Carlos laughed out loud but then immediately tried to cover it up with a coughing fit.

I would have laughed too, but the blood streaming out of Coach Earwax's nose looked too much like the Valentine's Day Schnoz Massacre.

CHAPTER 16

We spotted the Nike Preparatory School baseball stadium from two miles away. It was that big.

As we got closer, we could see on top of the scoreboard a gigantic sign: **Home of the Fighting Platypuses**.

Whah?

None of us, including Coach Earwax, had ever heard of a platypus. But the bus driver spoke up for the first time in the entire trip.

He must have been some kind of zoologist moonlighting as a bus driver.

Whoa! That is *way* cooler than a Mighty Plumber mascot.

Our bus pulled into the Nike Prep parking lot, and we were greeted by a man in a green blazer with a yellow tie.

We couldn't tell whether he was the school principal or a butler. He stood at attention outside the door of the bus and waited for us to exit.

Jimmy Jimerino immediately gave him the nickname Jeeves, which I hate to admit was sort of clever.

When we exited the bus, Jeeves greeted us with a stern look.

I couldn't tell if he meant watch your step getting off of the bus or watch your step as in "behave yourselves."

Nike Prep's stadium had skyboxes and a center-field scoreboard with a giant video screen. The only thing missing was a Goodyear blimp circling overhead.

It made the Mighty Plumbers stadium look like one of those ancient Greek ruins you see in history books.

Our dugout had a refrigerator stocked with imported bottled water and stacks of scented towels to wipe the chick-magnet sweat off our skin. A flat-screen TV monitor was mounted on the wall so that we could watch instant replays.

And the dugout had a cushioned bench!

One of Carlos's biggest complaints about sitting the pine is that wood benches are uncomfortable. And if you're not careful you can get a sliver stuck in your butt cheek.

(I had a teammate in youth leagues who got a sliver stuck in his rear end. He was too embarrassed to tell anyone, so he left it there for a week, hoping it would go away. But it got infected, and he had to drop his trousers at the doctor's office for an emergency sliver-ectomy.)

But Carlos was in heaven on the cushioned bench.

Becky O'Callahan was our starting pitcher. She and our catcher, Dominic Mumalo, walked out to the bullpen to warm up. (Nike Prep actually had bullpens just like the major leagues!)

Coach Earwax told us to take the field. We paired off to play catch and warm up our arms. Usually the other team also warms up.

Not the Platypuses.

The Nike Prep players marched out of their dugout single file in designer uniforms that looked like green-and-yellow space suits.

They didn't run. They didn't jog. They marched like robots onto the baseball diamond and circled the bases.

That was their pregame warm-up. It was both strange and awesome at the same time.

In the bullpen, Dominic Mumalo was like the rest of us—totally baffled by the Platypus marching routine. He stared at the bizarre parade and forgot all about catching Becky's first practice throw.

Her fastball nailed him right on the noggin. Fortunately, he was wearing his catcher's helmet, but when I saw it happen, what little confidence I had disappeared. It was another reminder of the Valentine's Day Schnoz Massacre.

CHAPTER 17

The game began, and we could tell right away that the Platypuses could march *way* better than they could play baseball.

Jimmy Jimerino hit a grand slam, a triple, and a double—and that was just in the first inning!

Meanwhile, Becky struck out every Nike Prep player who marched to the plate. She was awesome.

But the game itself was getting boring. So

Joey, Carlos, and I decided to kill time on the bench with one of our famous pranks.

We called the stadium announcer on the dugout phone. Carlos used his deep voice and asked the guy to page a spectator named Jacques Strapp.

About a minute later the poor, foolish stadium announcer made the announcement.

JOCK STRAP! WILL JOCK STRAP PLEASE REPORT TO THE TICKET BOOTH!!

The joke was on us, though. After the announcement a student sitting right next to our dugout ran toward the ticket booth. There really *was* someone named Jacques Strapp at Nike Prep!

Out on the field, the poor Platypuses

could not buy a hit in spite of their wealth.

It was a steady stream of strikeouts, ground outs, and pop-ups. And whenever we were up to bat, it was a merry-go-round of hits and runners scoring.

I actually started feeling sorry for the Platypuses. Like, maybe *they* were all suffering from Bean-O-Phobia?

Amazingly, Nike Prep did not seem to mind that they were getting creamed by the Mighty Plumbers.

Even the students in the stands were upbeat. They stood for the entire game and never stopped their annoying cheers while the Platypus mascot with the poisonous spurs cheerfully ran around and flapped its ducklike bill.

It was strange. The Nike Prep fans acted as if they were beating the pants off *us*!

All the cheerful noise really bugged Carlos, though, so he dug down deep into his gut and let loose one of his epic belches in order to quiet the crowd.

FRIENDS, ROMANS,
BOO-WAAAT!!
COUNTRYMEN. LEND
ME YOUR EARS!!

It was awesome.

The burp echoed across the field and frightened off some pigeons who were roosting on the scoreboard. But the happy-go-lucky Nike

Prep fans continued to clap and cheer.

By the eighth inning we were leading the Platypuses, a hundred to zip. It was garbage time. Every benchwarmer's dream!

Joey, Carlos, and I stared down the bench at Coach Earwax. He finally got the hint and nodded in our direction.

Translation: "Start warming up."

CHAPTER

In the bottom of the eighth we took the field—Carlos in left field, Joey at second base, and me in right field. It was good to get up off the bench, even if it was padded.

But we would have seen more action standing in the Nike Prep parking lot.

Becky was still working her magic. She struck out three Platypus batters with nine pitches. The inning was over before I had a chance to even adjust my athletic protector.

Carlos was happy, though. He sprinted off the field, into the dugout, and onto the padded bench.

Becky sat alone at the end of the bench. She was one inning away from pitching a no-hitter.

In baseball you can never say the word *no-hitter* before the final out or you will jinx everything. That's why Becky was sitting by herself. She did not want anyone to ruin her no-hitter accidentally.

Coach Earwax read the batting lineup: Joey at bat. Carlos on deck. Steve in the hole.

Way in the hole. I suddenly had one of those stomach things where it feels like your intestines are crawling out of your belly button.

The video in my mind started replaying the Valentine's Day Schnoz Massacre.

I closed my eyes and tried to picture something calm and pleasant. Like cheeseburgers or lizards.

All I could see was blood and Dewey's sideways nose.

Joey got to the plate, and Coach Earwax gave him the "take" sign.

That sly, top-secret sign meant Joey was supposed to just stand there like a garden gnome and let every pitch go by.

Yeah, I know. It sounds kind of dumb.

The whole purpose of going to bat is to hit the ball. But in Joey's case, because his strike zone is so tiny, there's an excellent chance that he will get on base with a walk.

Joey let three pitches go by, all balls. There is practically a rule in baseball that you *never* swing at the next pitch if your count is three balls and no strikes. Joey blew it off.

He bunted a high pitch and popped it up.

The Platypus pitcher and catcher both ran under the ball. That didn't work out so well.

Meanwhile, speedy Joey ran all the way around the bases and slid into home plate!

Unfortunately, before Joey touched home plate, the ball bounced off the pitcher's head and landed right in the pitcher's glove.

Out!

Pure luck.

Joey almost had a bunt homer!

Carlos lumbered up to the plate. The Platypuses were fooled by his big-boned body. The players all moved back in their positions. WAY back. I guess they thought that Carlos would crush the ball over the fence, out of the stadium, and into a far corner of the Earth.

Carlos dug his foot into the dirt in the back of the batter's box. Then he got into his stance and glared at the pitcher.

Carlos swung at the first pitch and whiffed. Strike one.

Second pitch, strike two.

He swung on the third pitch. Strike three!

Carlos stood in the batter's box for a moment and glared at his bat.

Carlos waddled back to the dugout and wiggled his butt down into the padded bench. That meant I was batter up.

Before I walked to the plate, Jimmy put an arm around my shoulder as if I was his best bud in the entire world. Jimmy was up to bat after me.

GET ON BASE, GOOSE EGG.

...OR ELSE!

Don't be fooled. Those were not words of encouragement.

Jimmy wanted another chance to boost his hotshot statistics with another home run.

So I not only had to worry about Bean-O-Phobia; I also had to fear the wrath of

Jimmy Jimerino and his posse if I failed to get on base.

Oh, and as I walked toward home plate? Jimmy added one more layer of stress.

At first I thought Jimmy was pulling one

of the oldest pranks in the entire universe. Then I looked down, and, sure enough, my pants zipper was wide open.

I was in big trouble. I couldn't stop and zip it up right there in front of hundreds of Nike Academy spectators. The only thing I could do was keep going and hope that no one would notice.

As soon as I stepped into the batter's box, the umpire called time-out and told me to step out of the batter's box. Then, in a loud voice, he told me to ZIP UP MY FLY.

Derp!

I tried to be all nonchalant about it, but it's pretty much impossible to look cool while zipping up your pants at home plate in front of hundreds of spectators.

The Platypus fans were polite. No one heckled me. Their catcher even turned his head away while I zipped up.

But I could hear Jimmy's posse cackling in the dugout. I looked over at Coach Ear-wax, and he scowled at me.

Translation: "Mighty Plumbers do not leave their zippers open!"

The wrath of Jimmy, public humiliation, *and* Bean-O-Phobia! My knees were shaking. My arms felt like rubber. It was a replay of every time I'd been to bat all season.

The pitcher threw the baseball, but, in my mind, I saw my recurring nightmare.

I hit the dirt.

The pitch was high and *way* outside, but I must have moved my bat in a forward motion on my way down because the umpire called a strike.

The rest of my time at bat was total darkness—probably because I had my eyes closed when I swung and whiffed on the next two pitches.

I was the last out. Inning over. Jimmy Jimerino never got his chance to hit another home run.

I had just pulled off probably the biggest batter meltdown in the entire history of baseball.

No brag. It's just a fact. Derp!

The walk back to the dugout seemed like it took forever. The Platypus fans were happy and cheering. The mascot ran around and flapped its duck bill.

My teammates ran back on the field for the Platypuses' last at bat. On his way out to shortstop, Jimmy made a point of giving me a personal stink eye.

Becky tapped me on the head on her way out to the mound. She looked back at me, and with Nature's Near-Perfect Smile she said:

"Shake it off, Steve."

Becky struck out three Platypus batters in a row to end the game. She got her no-hitter, and the Mighty Plumbers were headed for the Big Game: the League Championship.

Jimmy and his jock posse carried Becky off the field on their shoulders.

At the team bus, Jeeves stood at attention as we boarded for the ride back to Spiro. He greeted us with "Thank you for visiting Nike Preparatory Academy!"

Jeeves must have seen my humiliating meltdown at bat, because when I walked by, he gave me two encouraging words.

CHIN UP!!

I almost said, "Thank you, Jeeves." But that was a nice thing for him to say, and I didn't want him to think that I was being a wise guy hotshot athlete like Jimmy Jimerino.

On the way home my friends and I once again got stuck in the front row of the bus. This time I sat next to Coach Earwax.

He yanked nose hairs out of his nostrils all the way back to Spiro.

One more game to go. The Big Game. My last chance to break free of Bean-O-Phobia.

I would either get a hit or get Goosed.

CHAPTER

In the week leading up to the League Championship, I tried everything I could think of to break free of the Bean-O-Phobia. I even asked Carlos for advice, which was a waste of time. He told me that a phobia can be cured in *three easy steps*:

Sleep with a bat underneath my pillow.

Don't brush my teeth for a week.

Change the part in my hair from the left side to the right side.

Carlos was wrongity, wrong, wrong. I tried all three. Nothing worked, and sleeping with a bat under your pillow is really uncomfortable.

I decided to seek advice from a more reliable source: the Power Structure.

Parents are expert advisers if you're having a problem with fear. They deal with major phobias on a daily basis:

BAD BREATH

BALDNESS

CALORIES

Mom is a turbo-hyper-worrywart, so I went straight to my dad. I knew he might be able to offer some fear-free advice.

Quick Time-Out about Dad

Dad usually doesn't go to my games because he's either traveling on business or golfing, but that's okay with me. I actually get really nervous when he shows up.

I know I said I like being a benchwarmer, but I feel bad if my dad comes to a game and all I do is sit the pine and watch my coach dig wax out of his ears. And now, if a major miracle happened and I actually did get into the championship games, the dreaded Dad-O-Phobia would strike.

Dad-O-Phobia is a severe brain wreck that afflicts most people my age. Boys. Girls. It doesn't discriminate. You can be cruising along in a baseball game, not making any errors, then good old Father Figure shows up.

Dad-O-Phobia probably is an irrational fear, though. Most dads aren't all that scary. They just want to cheer and offer advice if you need it.

So I went to Dad for his advice and spilled my guts about Bean-O-Phobia.

I told him everything: Dewey's sideways nose, blood, gore, baseball the size of a meteor, my crush on Becky, open zipper at the plate, the Goose Egg.

Then I asked him if he knew of a cure for Bean-O-Phobia.

The open-zipper disaster gave Dad another one of his laughing fits. When he was done, he told me about a teammate in college who also struggled with Bean-O-Phobia.

The guy was so desperate, he tried a magic ritual to get rid of the fear. He stood on one leg and rubbed a chicken bone on his bat and chanted magic words:

He was supposed to rub the chicken bone on the bat in order to create powerful mojo, but instead he created a greasy mess because he forgot to remove the meat from the bone.

When he got up to the plate, he swung at the ball, and the bat slipped out of his hands and clobbered an umpire right in the shin, one of the most sensitive bones in the entire body.

Dad told me to stay away from magic rituals because they don't work. He tapped me on my noggin with his knuckles and said that the solution was right there—in my head.

He scribbled what he called a "Dr. Dad" prescription on the back of a golf scorecard and handed it to me. Dad told me to read it whenever I felt an attack of fear coming on.

I actually was more interested in the magic ritual with the chicken bone, but I kept Dad's cryptic note anyway.

CHAPTER 20

On the day of the Big Game I woke up with Fido curled on my chest as usual, flicking his tongue at my nose.

I jumped out of bed and instantly noticed two things:

First, I had a stiff neck. My mom had bought me a new "therapeutic" pillow that had the opposite effect. Apparently, she saw the bat under my old, thin pillow and worried that I might get a stiff neck from *that*.

I couldn't swivel my head. I had to turn my entire body in order to look left or right. I moved just like Frankenstein's monster. Derp!

And second, Fido had a guilty look on his face and a big bulge in his stomach. I looked closer and saw a scrap of paper hanging out the side of his mouth.

Brilliant. My math homework was halfway down his belly.

Fido felt bad, but it was all my fault. I usually feed him a mouse every two weeks, and I was a couple of days late.

When Fido's hungry, he'll swallow anything he can fit into his mouth: candy bars, hockey pucks, lightbulbs. One time he swallowed my cell phone.

It took a few days before Fido, er, *returned* my cell phone. But it still worked!

I took a shower and went into the laundry room to pull my baseball uniform out of the dryer. Dad was there, and *he* had a guilty look on his face.

Dad was holding a big pile of laundry in his arms. A pile of PINK laundry.

Including my formerly WHITE baseball uniform.

Dad pulled one of his bright-red golf socks out of the pile.

He had flunked Laundry 101: never wash white clothes with bright colors. There wasn't enough time to stick the uniform back in the wash to bleach out the pink, so I was stuck.

I have recurring nightmares about going to class wearing only my boxers. This was going to be far worse—and in real life. What a disaster.

Not only would I be pink at the game, I would be pink at school, because there's a tradition at Spiro that if a team makes the championships, players wear their jerseys to school on the day of a Big Game.

You're probably thinking it couldn't get much worse, but you'd be wrongity, wrong, wrong.

I couldn't find my athletic protector. I usually throw it in with the laundry, but it was missing.

I tore my bedroom apart looking for it: closet, drawers, mattress, snake terrarium.

IT WASN'T ME!
I'M FULL OF
HOMEWORK!!

The mystery was solved when Mom walked into my room. She was holding my missing cup between her thumb and forefinger as if it was a dead rat from our attic. It didn't even look like an athletic protector.

At least it wasn't pink.

So my mom flunked Garbage Disposal 101: check for foreign objects before you turn it on.

What a way to begin the day of the Big Game:

Frankenstein neck.

Snake ate my homework.

Pink uniform.

Demolished cup.

I put Fido back in his terrarium and left for school. But I had a feeling there was something I forgot.

CHAPTER

On the way to school I made a quick stop at O'Callahan's Sporting Goods. I was determined to defeat at least one of my fears that day.

Becky was not working, of course. She was in school. I ran in, grabbed an athletic protector, and strolled right up to the check-out counter.

It was painless! Mostly.

I got to Spiro and tried my best to blend in with the crowd in the carpeted hallways. I was worried that my pink jersey would attract a lot of attention.

I don't think anyone noticed.

My luck ran out at lunch in the cafeteria.

I should have been more cautious when I carried my food tray to C Central table, because Joey had just uttered a psychic warning.

Deck? Neck? Tech?

My Frankenstein stiff neck made it hard for me to look from side to side, and I walked right into the path of Becky O'Callahan, who was carrying *her* food tray.

Both of our trays flew up in the air. Plates shattered on the floor. Spaghetti splattered in all directions. The cafeteria crowd erupted in cheers and gave us a standing ovation.

Jimmy Jimerino and his posse at the Jock Table spotted my pink jersey and pounced.

I apologized to Becky and offered to get a towel to wipe off the spaghetti sauce that had splattered on her baseball jersey. But Becky smiled her Nature's Near-Perfect Smile and laughed it off.

Now we both had flawed jerseys. It was awesome.

CHAPTER

22

Finally the time came when I had to face my math teacher, Mr. Spleen, and explain why I did not have my homework. Everyone but me and Jimmy Jimerino turned in the assignment.

Jimmy and I were told to stay behind after class. I thought we would get the standard "everyone-else-in-the-class-turned-in-THEIR-homework" lecture, then we'd be on our way to the Big Game.

But nothing is that easy at Spiro T. Agnew Middle School.

Mother T. suddenly appeared out of nowhere in her spooky, ghostlike way. She stood there, hands folded prayer-like, and then she unleashed her mysterious mental powers.

She spoke softly about hardworking parents who provide food, clothing, and shelter while their knuckleheaded kids fail to turn in homework assignments on time. She said there are rules at Spiro that cannot be ignored. And one of the rules is that students absolutely cannot participate in games—even the Big Game—unless all homework is turned in.

Jimmy was stunned, but I have to admit that I almost knelt down at her feet to thank her for saving me from a last fateful clash with Bean-O-Phobia.

Mother T. offered a glimmer of hope, though. She told Mr. Spleen that he could

overlook the missing homework assignment if he thought there was an "acceptable
excuse."

As quickly as Mother T. had appeared,
she was gone!

THANK YOU,
MOTHER T.
I WILL...
HELLO??

Our fate was in the hands of Mr. Spleen.
He asked Jimmy why he did not have his
algebra homework. As always, Jimmy was
confident his BJOC status would protect
him.

Jimmy launched into a far-fetched story
about how he was in the gym lifting weights
the night before the Big Game and afterward

he was so exhausted that he could not even lift a pencil.

Wow. What a pathetic excuse. Completely bogus.

So naturally, Mr. Spleen swallowed the whole tale and let Jimmy Jimerino the hotshot athlete completely off the hook.

Jimmy strutted out of the classroom, and under his breath he said, "See ya later . . . Goose Egg."

After watching Jimmy get away with his lame story, I figured my honest and understandable "the snake ate my homework" excuse would be fine with Mr. Spleen.

I'VE HEARD THAT EXCUSE A MILLION TIMES! A MILLION TIMES!!

But . . .

He offered me one final chance to redeem myself. Mr. Spleen scribbled on the board a mind-boggling equation from some alien planet. Probably Pluto.

If I solved it, I could play in the Big Game.

I looked at the equation. All I could think about was the Goose Egg.

I had one minute.

Time ticked away. All was lost. I buried my head in my arms and mumbled something about Bean-O-Phobia and Goose Egg and a baseball season without getting even one hit.

Mr. Spleen was totally bumfuzzled.

He pointed to the door. I was free to go.

To the Big Game!

CHAPTER

I sprinted to the locker room and put on the rest of my uniform. I put on my cleats and baseball cap. Then I reached into my gear bag and discovered that I hadn't followed Dad's "ninety percent preparation" rule.

I forgot my glove.

Derp!

The team headed out of the locker room for the field. I didn't have much time.

I would have asked Joey to run and fetch my glove, because he would be back in about thirty seconds and I'm not even exaggerating. But Joey had already dashed like a flea to the field way ahead of everyone else.

I had no choice. I ducked out the back door of the locker room and sprinted for home.

It was awkward running in cleats on cement sidewalks, and it made a really loud racket that attracted all kinds of attention.

I ran into the house and grabbed my glove. On the way out of the room, I glanced at the terrarium. The lid was open, and there was no sign of Fido.

I thought maybe he was just doing his free-range thing, so I looked all over the house: kitchen, laundry room, family room, Mom's bathtub.

No Fido. He was gone.

There was no time to spare. I had to get to the game and hope that Fido would free-range himself right back into his terrarium.

I sprinted all the way back to school and made it to the stadium just as the Mighty Plumbers were running onto the field.

If I had been a starting player, Coach Earwax would have noticed that I was late. But benchwarmers become pretty much invisible at game time. Besides, Coach was a little distracted.

I slipped unseen onto the bench.

CHAPTER 24

The Chaney Middle School Werewolves were our opponents for the League Championship. And, yeah, they were a scary team.

I don't live in a tough part of town. We've got a couple of abandoned buildings, and a few years ago someone dumped detergent in the central park fountain and suds spilled out onto Seventh Street. But that's about as tough as it gets.

The Werewolves were from a *really* tough part of town where even Mother T. would have had a hard time keeping the peace. We were told Chaney Middle School has uniformed guards and front doors made of steel and cement walls that are three feet thick. It's practically a fortress built to withstand anarchy or barbarian invaders.

The Werewolves had a reputation for poor sportsmanship and for starting a brawl if you even looked at them the wrong way.

Before the game, Coach Earwax instructed

us to avoid eye contact if a Werewolves player confronted us. And, if threatened, we were to roll into a fetal position and pretend to be dead.

We were all worried, but the game got off to a good start. Becky was pitching, and for the first five innings she had another no-hitter going—even with the spaghetti stains on her jersey.

But Skinny Dennis forgot about the no-hitter jinx rule. He told Becky she was "bombdiggity" because she hadn't allowed a hit.

The very next batter lined a double to left field, and that was the end of Becky's no-hitter.

The game was still scoreless in the seventh inning. I think the Werewolves were beginning to wonder if their scary reputation had lost its effect, because they brought in a Secret Weapon.

Our stadium announcer introduced the new Werewolves pitcher, but he made the mistake of using his real name.

NOW PITCHING...
BIFFY LeBOUF!

Biffy gave the announcer a scary Werewolves stink eye. He was quickly reintroduced by his preferred nickname:

ER... NOW
PITCHING...
BEAST!

Beast was probably six feet ten inches tall, and I am not even exaggerating. He had freakishly thick arms and stringy hair that spilled out the back of his baseball cap like tentacles.

The Werewolves crowd chanted all deep-throated and scary as he lumbered like Godzilla out to the mound.

Beast threw blazing fastballs with little or no control. In the dirt. Wide right. Wide left. Way, way, WAY high.

All game long I had been hoping for one last chance at bat, but I lost my enthusiasm after watching Beast warm up. Maybe I could live with the Goose Egg after all.

Our first batter was Tommy Hanks, who was the second-smallest player on the team and the starting second baseman, ahead of Joey.

Beast threw his blazing fastball to Hanks, and the ball skipped in the dirt and ricocheted right into his shin, which as you know is one of the most sensitive bones in the entire body.

Tommy was carried off the field on a stretcher. He was done.

Coach Earwax looked over at the bench. He motioned for Joey to go in for Tommy and take his place at first base as the pinch runner.

Our next batter was Otto Bertolero, our center fielder. When Otto stepped into the batter's box, Joey went into psychic mode all the way from his spot on first base.

Seconds later, Beast threw another fast-ball way inside. The ball smacked Otto right in the lower back.

P.S. Getting hit by a fastball in the kidney is almost more painful than getting hit in the shin. Poor Otto took a ride to the doctor in Mr. Joseph's filthy pickup truck.

Coach Earwax said he had to show "an abundance of caution."

Coach Earwax looked over at the bench for another pinch runner. You could tell he was struggling to decide what player to put in the game in place of Otto. Who does he choose: Pink Goose Egg or Big-Bone Malcontent?

He chose Carlos.

I didn't need Joey to predict what would happen next. After watching two players get clobbered by Beast, the next three Mighty Plumber batters were stricken with Bean-O-Phobia.

They closed their eyes and swung wildly at every pitch. Three batters up, three strike-outs. Suddenly, I didn't feel so alone in the world.

CHAPTER 25

At the start of the ninth inning, with the game scoreless, the Mighty Plumbers took the field. Joey was at second base and Carlos was in center field. I sat on the pine.

Beast was the first batter up. I think Becky was trying to do a little payback, because her first pitch was high and inside. That probably was a bad decision.

Beast hit the dirt. He got back up and was so mad you could practically see smoke coming out of his ears and nostrils.

Beast swung at Becky's next pitch and drilled the ball deep to right field. Skinny Dennis backpedaled as fast as he could. Back, back. Way back.

A little TOO far back.

Skinny Dennis was out cold. The ball bounced off the fence, and Beast made it all the way to second base.

Coach Earwax helped load Skinny into Mr. Joseph's filthy pickup truck for the "abundance of caution" trip to the doctor.

Coach looked over at the bench. He was down to one replacement. No other choice. He gave me "the nod."

I ran out to right field and got into proper position, with weight on the balls of my feet and my knees bent. Then I mentally prepared myself for action.

Becky struck out two Werewolves in a row. I was pretty sure that she was going to strike out the next batter, so I sort of lost focus and glanced over at the bleachers.

Dad was at the game!

He was sitting next to my mom, and when Dad saw me look over he waved. Instantly, I was struck with Dad-O-Phobia. My stomach did a somersault. My legs shook.

I tried as hard as I could to fight off a total dork meltdown right in the middle of the Big Game. I was trying so hard, I didn't see the Werewolves batter hit the first pitch.

I picked up the ball and threw it as hard as I could toward home, but Beast had already scored from second base.

Becky struck out the next batter, but the damage was done. The Werewolves were ahead, 1–0.

The Mighty Plumbers slouched off the field. Joey and I tried to get Carlos to belt out one of his famous burps to boost team morale, but his guts were all tied up in knots because of Beast.

CHAPTER 26

The Mighty Plumbers had one last turn at bat. The timing could not have been worse.

JOEY AT BAT. CARLOS ON DECK. AND [GULP!] STEVE IN THE HOLE.

Joey went to bat and tried to bunt, but he popped it up to Beast, who caught it easily.

Carlos belted a shot deep into left field, but it drifted foul. Then he struck out.

My moment of truth had arrived.

I looked over at the bench from the on-deck circle. Everyone's faces were glum—all except Becky's. She smiled That Smile and gave me a thumbs-up.

Jimmy was up after me. He told me, "Get on base, Goose Egg." Or else.

I walked over to the batter's box. The catcher, er, complimented me on my pink jersey.

The Bean-O-Phobia video began playing in my mind: Blood. Sideways nose. Baseball the size of a meteor. The first pitch came right at my head. I dove into the dirt. When I got up, my knees were shaking.

The next pitch was high and way outside, but I closed my eyes and swung anyway. Derp!

I had two strikes with two outs, and my team was behind by a run in the final inning of the League Championship.

I stepped out of the batter's box and pulled my dad's FEAR prescription out of my back pocket.

I took a deep breath and looked up into the bleachers.

The entire Spiro student body and faculty—all dressed in teal-colored clothing—

were on their feet and hoping for a miracle. Even Mother T. was there with her hands folded as if in prayer.

I stepped back into the batter's box. Beast grinned at me. I think he was drooling.

I blocked Beast out of my mind and focused on hitting the baseball.

Forget Everything And Relax.

No fear!

Beast threw a fastball right down the middle. I kept my eyes wide open. The ball seemed to be as big as a meteor! I didn't actually swing. It was more like I just stuck the bat out over the plate, and it collided with the ball.

I hit a soft blooper over the third baseman's head. It landed in front of the left fielder, and he picked it up, then bobbled the ball. By the time he got hold of it again, I was running for second base. In his panic, the fielder made a bad throw, and I sprinted for third.

I knew it was going to be a close play, so I

pulled off one of my excellent headfirst slides into the bag.

No brag. It's just a fact.

The home crowd erupted in cheers. Mom and Dad jumped up and down and hugged each other. Mother T. actually cracked a smile.

On the bench, Mighty Plumbers bumped chests and slapped hands.

Coach Earwax helped me up at third base. I was sweating like a hotshot athlete and covered from head to toe in dirt. It was awesome.

And I think Coach Earwax really meant
it.

My Bean-O-Phobia was conquered—and
the Goose Egg was smashed!

CHAPTER 27

The fate of the Mighty Plumbers now was in the hands of Jimmy Jimerino.

A base hit would tie the score. A home run would win the game and the League Championship. Hotshot athletes like Jimmy Jimerino dream of these high-pressure moments.

He stepped into the batter's box. He was brimming with confidence. Beast glared at

Jimmy. Jimmy made direct eye contact and glared right back at Beast.

Right about then I saw something move in the grass in front of home plate. A small head popped up and looked around.

Fido!

My free-range snake had followed me all the way to the ball field! I think he was full of guilt for eating my homework, and he wanted to apologize.

Just as Beast was going into his windup, Jimmy Jimerino spotted Fido in the grass. Jimmy's eyes bulged. His legs shook. His arms turned to rubber.

Textbook case of Snake-O-Phobia.

Jimmy scrunched down into a fetal position just as Beast unleashed a blazing fastball.

Jimmy's bat was sticking up over his head. The ball hit the bat and dribbled like a puny Pee Wee league bunt right to the pitcher's mound.

Beast bent over and picked up the ball with his bare hand. Then he walked—walked!—over to where Jimmy was cowering at the plate.

Jimmy was tagged out. The game was over. The Chaney Middle School Werewolves were League Champions.

I ran over and scooped up Fido. I stuffed him down my shirt before he could do any more emotional damage to Jimmy.

The Mighty Plumbers quietly gathered up their gear. No one said a word to Jimmy— not even his hotshot athlete posse.

Everyone was left wondering: what happened to Jimmy Jimerino?

Only me and Jimmy and Fido knew the truth.

Becky walked over to Jimmy and patted him on the back. Translation: shake it off.

She turned to me and flashed Nature's Near-Perfect Smile. Then Becky gave me a big hug, right in front of Jimmy, and winked!

My knees did not wobble. I was solid as cement. I smiled right back at Becky O'Callahan.

The Mighty Plumbers shuffled off the field. Jimmy and I were alone in the dugout.

I walked over and stuck out my hand. Jimmy hesitated, then he shook hands. I told him not to feel bad. Everyone struggles with some kind of fear.

I don't know if he had expected me to make some sarcastic remark or if he was still in Snake-O-Phobia shock, but Jimmy just stared at me wide-eyed and didn't say a word. (Fido tried to crawl out of my shirt to mess with Jimmy's brain, but I quickly shoved him back in.)

Mom and Dad were waiting for me by the bleachers. Dad swatted me on the butt the way hotshot athletes always do. Mom gave me a big hug and a sloppy kiss the way moms always do.

Then she wiped the lipstick off my face with her germy spit.

I would have ridden home with my parents, but there was one more thing I needed to do.

I went into the Mighty Plumbers' locker room. Not once during the entire season did I take a shower after practice or games, because ace benchwarmers like me rarely get dirty and drenched in chick-magnet sweat.

So it felt good when I hopped in the shower, lathered up with soap, and finally was able to wash actual dirt and sweat right down the drain.

And along with it any remaining trace of Bean-O-Phobia.

EPILOGUE

I wasn't exactly the hotshot athlete hero of the Big Game, but I did single-handedly defeat the humiliating phobia that almost ruined my first baseball season at Spiro T. Agnew Middle School.

And like I already told you, I don't even want to be a BJOC like Jimmy Jimerino.

You've got to win at everything, and who needs that kind of pressure?

I'm fine with sitting on the bench—at least for now.

Besides, I'm probably better at it than anyone else my age in the entire universe. End of the pine. Middle of the pine. Doesn't matter.

I'm King of the Bench!

No brag. It's just a fact.